W9-ARA-134

PALM BEACH COUNTY
LIBRARY SYSTEM
3650 Summit Boulevard
West Palm Beach, FL 33406-4198

PETAL AND POPPY AND THE MYSTERY VALENTINE

LISA CLOUGH
AND
ED BRIANT

Green Light Readers
HOUGHTON MIFFLIN HARCOURT
Boston New York

Text copyright © 2014 by Lisa Clough
Illustrations copyright © 2014 by Ed Briant

All rights reserved. Green Light Readers® and its logo are trademarks of HMH Publishing LLC, registered in the United States and other countries.

For information about permission to reproduce selections from this book, write to Permissions, Houghton Mifflin Harcourt Publishing Company, 215 Park Avenue South, New York, New York 10003.

www.hmhco.com

The text of this book is set in Cheltenham.
The display type was hand-lettered.
The illustrations were created digitally.

The Library of Congress Cataloging-in-Publication Data
Jahn-Clough, Lisa.
Petal and Poppy and the mystery valentine / by Lisa Clough and Ed Briant.
p. cm. — (Green light readers. Level 3)
Summary: On Valentine's Day morning, Petal the elephant wakes up to find chocolates and Poppy the rhinocerous finds flowers, but they forgot to get gifts for each other, so who is their mystery Valentine?
ISBN 978-0-544-55549-5 paperback
ISBN 978-0-544-55550-1 paper over board
[1. Valentines Day—Fiction. 2. Best friends—Fiction. 3. Friendship—Fiction. 4. Elephants—Fiction. 5. Rhinoceroses—Fiction.] I. Briant, Ed, illustrator. II. Title.
PZ7.J153536Pfk 2015
[E]—dc23
2014037904

Manufactured in China
SCP 10 9 8 7 6 5 4 3 2 1

4500554164

Zzzz . . .
Zzzz . . .

Will I get a valentine today?
FEBRUARY
14

Pretty flowers! I did get a valentine!

Hmm . . .
no name.

They must be
from Poppy.

Uh-oh. I forgot
to get something
for Poppy!

Will I get a valentine today?
FEBRUARY
14

Yummy chocolates! I did get a valentine!

Hmm . . . no name.
They must be from Petal.
Uh-oh! I forgot to get something for Petal!

Thank you for the Valentine's gift!

Should I tell her I forgot?

Um . . . Petal . . .
Yes, Poppy?
I did not get you anything.
I did not get you anything either.
So who gave me flowers?
And who gave me chocolates?

Was it a secret admirer?
Or was it a stranger?
KNOCK!
KNOCK!
Aaaah!
Aaaah!

What is it?
Another valentine.
No name.
It is a mystery.

A mystery valentine.
Who could it be?
I bet it really is Poppy.
I bet it really is Petal.
No idea.

Look.
Another one.

No name.

The mystery valentine strikes again.

And another.

Here too.

The mystery valentine is very busy.
These could be clues.
Let's follow them.

It is snowing valentines!

Look up there!
What is it?

It must be the mystery valentine!
In a big red balloon!

If you are down here, then you cannot be the mystery valentine.
Nope.

And you cannot be the mystery valentine either.
Nope.

Help!
What can we do with all of these valentines?

I have an idea.
What?
We can give the cards away.

To everyone we love.

Here is a treat!
This is for you!

You are so sweet!
Yes, it is true . . .
We love you, too!

I love you, Poppy!
I love you, Petal!
We have no more cards.
Time to go home.

Look who is here!
MYSTERY VALENTINE
I think he wants us to follow.
MYSTERY VALENTINE

Aha! This is the valentine balloon!
Aha! You are the mystery valentine!

Thank you!
Thank you!
Up we go!
Wait for me!

Everyone is happy.
With help from the mystery valentine, of course.

The best mystery valentine . . .
. . . in the world.

You are sweet!
You are lovely!
Happy Valentine's Day!